W9-AZC-614

Baseball

FOR BREAKFAST

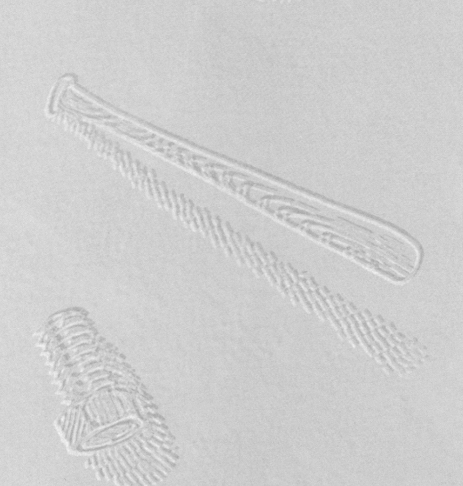

*"And we know that in all things
God works for the good of those
who love him, who have been called
according to his purpose."*

ROMANS 8:28 (NIV)

Baseball for Breakfast: The Story of a Boy Who Hated to Wait
Text Copyright © 1999 Bill Myers
Illustrations Copyright © 1999 Frank Riccio

All rights reserved. No portion of this book may be reproduced in any form
without the written permission of the publisher, except for brief excerpts in
reviews.

Library of Congress Cataloging–in–Publication Data

Myers, Bill, 1953–
     Baseball for breakfast : the story of a boy who hated to wait / written by
Bill Myers ; illustrated by Frank Riccio.
         p.   cm.
     Summary: When Jimmy finds an unusual pocket watch that lets him skip
ahead in time, he does only the things he thinks are fun, but he soon discovers
the wisdom of God's plan for us to experience both the good times and the bad.
     ISBN 0–8499–5871–7
     [1. Time—Fiction. 2. Christian life—Fiction. 3. Patience—Fiction.] I.
Riccio, Frank, ill. II. Title.
PZ7.M98234Bas   1999
[Fic]—dc21

99–12182
CIP

Printed in the United States of America
99 00 01 02 03 RRD 9 8 7 6 5 4 3 2 1

Baseball

FOR BREAKFAST

THE STORY OF A BOY WHO HATED TO WAIT

BILL MYERS

ILLUSTRATED BY FRANK RICCIO

Tommy
NELSON

Thomas Nelson, Inc.
Nashville

PUBLIC LIBRARY, PLAINFIELD, NJ

Jimmy hated to wait. He hated waiting to finish dinner so he could eat dessert. He hated waiting for recess. But most of all, he hated waiting for the rain to stop so he could go outside and play baseball.

"It's just not fair," he complained to his mother as he put on his pajamas. "Why do we always have to wait for the good times? Why can't the good times happen right away?"

"Because God has made *all* times important," his mother said. "The good times, the bad times, and the in–between times."

"I don't understand," Jimmy said, scrunching his forehead into a frown.

His mother smiled. "If you had your way, you wouldn't wait for a thing. Why, you'd play baseball all the time. You'd play it for lunch, dinner, even for breakfast."

"What's wrong with that?" Jimmy asked.

His mother laughed softly. "You may not understand now, but wait until you are a little older, and it will make more sense." Then she tenderly kissed him, reminded him to say his prayers, and said goodnight.

As Jimmy closed his eyes, the words burned in his heart. *Wait, wait, wait, that's all everyone wants me to do. Mom's right. If I were in charge, I'd make sure I'd never have to wait for another thing ever again.*

As those thoughts tumbled and turned inside his head, Jimmy drifted off to sleep.

Before he knew it, he was heading back to school. On the way he found a very unusual pocket watch. Oh, he didn't notice it was unusual at first, but when he tried to set the time, something very odd happened. By moving the minute hand just a little bit forward, he was no longer walking to school. Instead, he was already sitting inside his classroom! Somehow, he had skipped ten whole minutes of time.

Amazing!

As his teacher, Mrs. Peterson, greeted the class, Jimmy reached down and again moved the watch hands forward.

Suddenly, Mrs. Peterson was taking role. He moved the watch hands forward again, and she was writing on the blackboard. When he moved them a little more, the recess bell was ringing.

How incredible. By moving the pocket watch hands forward, he could actually skip ahead through time!

When the class returned from recess, Jimmy could hardly wait for lunch. But why wait? He turned the watch hands forward to noon. The bell rang, and to everyone's surprise, it was time for lunch. Soon they were all racing down the hallway to the cafeteria.

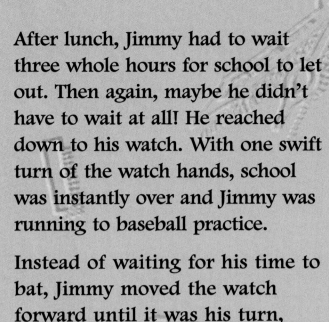

After lunch, Jimmy had to wait three whole hours for school to let out. Then again, maybe he didn't have to wait at all! He reached down to his watch. With one swift turn of the watch hands, school was instantly over and Jimmy was running to baseball practice.

Instead of waiting for his time to bat, Jimmy moved the watch forward until it was his turn, and then forward again until it was his turn again, and then forward some more. Before anyone knew it, practice was over and Jimmy had been the only one up to bat!

"Hey! What happened to us?" a teammate shouted.

"Yeah," the others cried. "How did we miss our turn?"

"Oh, well," Jimmy grinned. "Guess you'll have to start paying better attention."

"That's not fair!" they complained. "How come you got to—"

But that was all Jimmy wanted to hear. Before they finished their grumbling, he reached down, moved the watch hands forward, and he was back at home.

At dinner, Jimmy didn't have to clean his plate before getting dessert. He simply moved the watch hands until, suddenly, he was eating a delicious hot fudge sundae!

And, since he hated homework, he moved the hands forward until he could go outside and play flashlight tag with his friends.

The next day he decided to skip school altogether.
He set the watch for baseball practice. But, since
practice wasn't as much fun as the actual games, he
was soon skipping ahead to only the days they played
their games . . . and, of course, to only the times he was
up to bat.

There were other advantages, too. Like never having to sit through another haircut, or take another bath, or be dragged from store to store by his mother to shop for clothes. And when the rainy days came, Jimmy simply skipped past them until it was sunny again.

It looked like Jimmy would never have to wait for another thing. Never again would he have to experience the bad times or the in–between times. Now there would only be good times—one after another after another.

Yes sir, things could not have been better. Or could they . . . ?

It wasn't too long before Jimmy started to grow very weak. Soon he was so weak he could barely drag himself to his baseball games. And, once he was there, he was too weak to hold the bat. He had no choice but to let the other players take their turns at the plate. But since he had never allowed them to practice, no one ever scored a run. The team began losing every game!

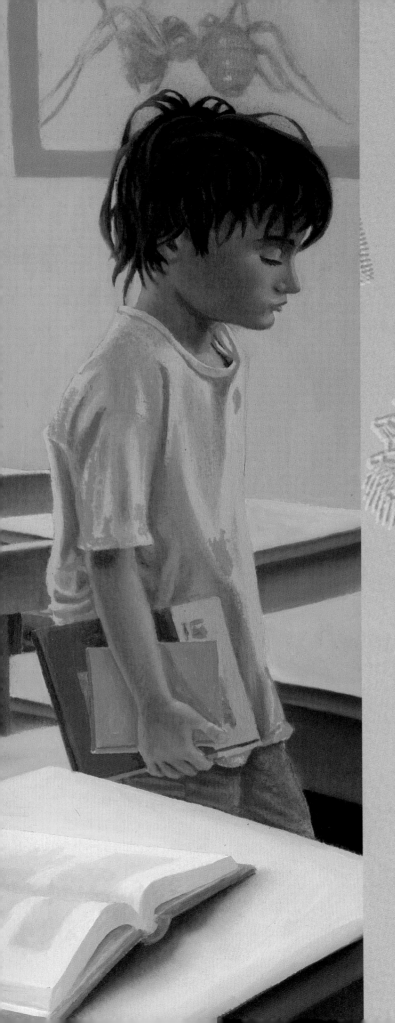

And, since Jimmy always skipped past his study time at home, he was no longer one of the best students in class. In fact, he began to fail every subject!

But there was more. Since he always skipped past his time for haircuts, clothes shopping, and taking baths, he began to look so messy, his clothes grew so ragged, and he smelled so terrible that no one would go near him.

"Who's wearing the birdnest hat?" they cried.

"That's just Jimmy!"

"Who's the scarecrow?"

"That's just Jimmy!"

"Whew, is somebody eating rotten eggs?"

"That's just Jimmy!"

It wasn't too long before everyone in the entire school was laughing at him.

Finally, there was the weather. By only enjoying the sunny days and skipping the rainy ones, a terrible drought spread across the land. Plants withered and died. Farmers could no longer raise crops. Soon there wouldn't be any food.

And everyone knew who was to blame. They all gathered under Jimmy's bedroom window and began yelling and screaming.

"We're losing our games because of you!" his teammates shouted.

"You won't pass if you don't do your work," Mrs. Peterson warned.

"You are the weirdest person we've ever seen!" his friends yelled.

"Because of you there is no food!" the farmers cried.

By now Jimmy was so weak he could barely move. "Mom, why is everything going so wrong?"

"Honey, with your pocket watch, you are living only in the good times. By refusing to wait, you are skipping all the bad and in–between times."

"But why is that wrong? Why does everyone hate me? And why am I so weak that I can hardly move?"

"All of your questions have the same answer. You are weak because you skip past your meals to dessert. You skip all the in–between foods of meat and fruits and vegetables."

"They don't taste as good," he protested.

"But they are the foods that give you your strength," she said.

And it was that loud crash that woke Jimmy up!

It had only been a dream. The watch was gone. The shouting crowd had disappeared. Now there was only silence . . . except for the morning rain as it lightly pattered against his bedroom window.

He threw back his covers and moved to the window for a better look. He peered through the glass and watched the rain. He wasn't sure if baseball practice would be canceled for the day or not, but it really didn't matter.

After all, rainy days were just a part of the life God had planned—a life to be lived in the good times, the bad times, and most importantly, in all of the in–between times.

Besides, he thought as he watched a faint rainbow spread across the sky, *all of this rain will be great for puddle splashing.*

"Why are my friends and my teacher and all those people down there so mad at me?"

"It's exactly the same as when you skip past your meals to dessert," his mother said. "When you skip the bad and in-between times of life, when you refuse to live each moment as God has planned, you destroy *all* the moments, including the good ones."

"But what do I do? How can I make the good moments come back?"

"You must live *every* moment. The good moments, the bad moments, and all the in-between moments. Each one is there for a reason, Jimmy. And only by living each moment will you truly be able to live."

Jimmy looked at his watch and began to nod. "I think I understand," he answered softly. "Life is more than just eating dessert and playing baseball on sunny days. It's also eating your vegetables and having to stay inside when it rains."

His mother nodded.

"What can I do to make things right, Mom?"

"You must destroy the watch, Jimmy. You must never skip another moment again."

It was a difficult decision, but slowly, painfully, Jimmy raised the watch. After taking a deep breath, he used all of his strength to fling it out of the open window and onto the sidewalk, where it shattered into a thousand pieces.